Dear Parents,

Welcome to the Scholastic Reader series. We have taken over 80 years of experience with teachers, parents, and children and put it into a program that is designed to match your child's interests and skills.

Level 1—Short sentences and stories made up of words kids can sound out using their phonics skills and words that are important to remember.

Level 2—Longer sentences and stories with words kids need to know and new "big" words that they will want to know.

Level 3—From sentences to paragraphs to longer stories, these books have large "chunks" of texts and are made up of a rich vocabulary.

Level 4—First chapter books with more words and fewer pictures.

It is important that children learn to read well enough to succeed in school and beyond. Here are ideas for reading this book with your child:

- Look at the book together. Encourage your child to read the title and make a prediction about the story.
- Read the book together. Encourage your child to sound out words when appropriate. When your child struggles, you can help by providing the word.
- Encourage your child to retell the story. This is a great way to check for comprehension.
- Have your child take the fluency test on the last page to check progress.

Scholastic Readers are designed to support your child's efforts to learn how to read at every age and every stage. Enjoy helping your child learn to read and love to read.

— **Francie Alexander**
Chief Education Officer
Scholastic Education

To Ian M. Nagel,
with love and thanks for all your ideas.
—K.B.N.

For Robin
—B.S.

Text copyright © 1992 by Karen Nagel.
Illustrations copyright © 1992 by Brian Schatell.
Activities copyright © 2003 Scholastic Inc.

All rights reserved. Published by Scholastic Inc.
SCHOLASTIC, CARTWHEEL BOOKS, and associated logos are trademarks and/or registered trademarks of Scholastic Inc.

ISBN 0-590-44972-9

Library of Congress Cataloging-in-Publication Data is available.

40 39   17 18 19/0

Printed in the U.S.A.   40
First printing, April 1992

Two Crazy Pigs

by Karen Berman Nagel
Illustrated by Brian Schatell

Scholastic Reader — Level 2

SCHOLASTIC INC.

New York   Toronto   London   Auckland   Sydney
Mexico City   New Delhi   Hong Kong   Buenos Aires

We are two crazy pigs.
We lived on the
Fenster farm.

We tickled the hens while
they were laying eggs.

"Stop that, you crazy pigs,"
yelled Mr. Fenster.

We tied the cows' tails together while they were giving milk.

"Stop that, you crazy pigs,"
yelled Mrs. Fenster.

Instead of rolling in the mud,
we threw it at each other.

OOPS!

"Pack your bags and leave!"
yelled Mr. and Mrs. Fenster.

All the animals cried, "We'll miss you, crazy pigs!"

We went down the road to
Mr. and Mrs. Henhawk's farm.
"Do you have room here for
two crazy pigs?" we asked.

Mr. Henhawk made us a new
pigpen.

He laughed when we dipped
the sheep's tail in ink.

Mrs. Henhawk let us make
mud pies in her stove.

One day the Fensters' cow,
Shirley, came to visit.

"Will you come back to the
farm?" Shirley asked.

"The hens are not laying eggs.

The cows have stopped
giving milk."

"No," we said. "Mr. and
Mrs. Henhawk love us for
who we are — crazy pigs."

We pulled Shirley's tail and
said good-bye. Then she went
back to the Fenster farm.

One week later, all of the Fensters' animals came to the Henhawk farm.

Shirley spoke.
"The Fensters have moved to
the city. Do you have room
for us here?"

Mr. and Mrs. Henhawk asked all the animals to live on their farm.

We were very happy to have our friends back.

We rubbed everybody's faces in mud.

We jumped on the Henhawks'
feather bed for two hours.

We were so happy! "Let's visit the Fensters in the city for old time's sake," we said.

"Are you kidding?" asked
Shirley.
"Are you sure?" asked
Mr. Henhawk.

"No," we said, "we're crazy!"